Simply, Wisdom

Simply, Wisdom

Alice M. Peoples

To order additional copies of this book, contact:
Xlibris
1-888-795-4274
www.Xlibris.com
Orders@Xlibris.com
778549

TABLE OF CONTENTS

ACKNOWLEDGEMENTS

Thanks to family and friends for your inspiration,
encouragement, and support in writing this book of love.

It has been a blessing to share the sweet and wonderful memories
of a truly magnificent wife, mother, friend, and super woman.

May all who read this book grow in Grace.

Special thanks to all for assisting me in completing this magical project.

Special thanks to my husband John for his support.

ABOUT THE AUTHOR

Alice White-Peoples, the author, resides in Oklahoma
City with her husband and two grandsons.

She enjoys cooking, traveling, and gardening;
these are a few of her favorite things.

Alice is a retired educator and administrator
with the Detroit Public Schools.

She is the mother of three; two daughters and
one son; and the grandmother of four.

PREFACE

This book is dedicated to the memories of my loving
mother, Velma Hampton, who taught us how to live
in Christ and be productive in the world!

She was the epitome of a Proverbs 31 Woman,
A Virtuous Woman.

I will forever reflect on the beautiful memories that she left behind.

Rest in His arms;
Your work on earth

INTRODUCTION

Wisdom is defined as, "the quality of having experience, knowledge, and good judgment, the quality of being wise." Only a Godly mother could possess the unique qualities, listed above.

To have lived in the presence of such a respected and outstanding woman, is to possess the wisdom of Solomon and the faith of Esther.

Mama Biggs or Big Ma (as she was affectionately called by family) was self sacrificing, humble, intelligent, kind-hearted, generous, witty, quiet-spirited, and of strong faith. She could entertain strangers, sit with kings and queens, and still praise and dance with the angels in heaven, as I believe she is doing today.

Mama walked the walk and talked the talk. To know and see her was to love in action; and, was better than anyone could imagine.

This book is written to share common sense wisdom that will hopefully help to enlighten and strengthen women to become more joyous and selective in their relationships and more confident within themselves.

We are in this world, but not of this world. Our success in life, depends on how we interact with one another. Do we want what others have? Do we criticize each other because we are afraid to launch out and become risk takers to fulfill our dreams and desires? As believers in Christ Jesus, we are to "Encourage one another and build each other up, just as in fact you are doing." 1 Thessalonians 5:11, NIV 3.

Life is short and love is sweet, but both can hurt. Even a mother's love can only last for a season. We need to understand that we will leave our loved ones, or they will leave us before we are prepared for this thing called "life." But, oh, the sweet memories that a Godly mother leaves behind are priceless, and they are passed down from one generation to another until the end of time; and, you know what, there is enough wisdom to enlighten a whole new world.

Great women raise Great women who raise Great women. (Hallmark plaque, 2012)

May all who read this book be blessed! (Hallmark plaque, 2019)

Mama

"A THING OF BEAUTY IS A JOY FOREVER"
John Keats

Her eyes sparked like diamonds in silver
sockets on a black starry night and her smile
always warmed you through and through!
A room would light up with her presence.

Her hair was long and silkier than a horse's mane.

A mother is always one of the most
humble and beauty person.

All mothers possess beauty.

Mother had the leadership of Moses,

The courage of Daniel,

and

The patience of Job,

and

The love of GOD!

Mothers are traffic lights, yield and stop signs,
road repairs, and they proceed with caution. They
are encouragers, steadfast, and self-sacrificing.
Godly mothers are generous, witty,
quiet spirits and devoted.
Mothers are leaders and children are followers.
Mothers help to prevent injuries and fatal accidents
(if you listen and follow directions).

Daddy, Sidney L Sr. and Mama, Velma

Mama

Always Busy as

the Board of Education,

Hospital,

Police Department,

Fire Department,

Guidance Counselor,

Finance Department,

Department of Recreation,

Domestic Engineer

Santa Claus, and

Angel of Forgiveness

"I can do all things through Christ who strengthens me."
Phil 4:13

Mama always wore a SMILE!

Smiles discourage wrinkles.

L to R: Eddis, Sid, Author, Ron, Millie, and Willie

Alice and Mama

One

can travel the world

without leaving home!

Increase your knowledge while

relaxing your mind.

Visit your local library often!

Reading is knowledge!

"Now therefore ye are no more strangers and foreigners, but fellow citizens with the saints, and of the household of faith." Ephesians 2:19

L to R: Ron, Millie, Willie, Author, and Bishop Hampton

Hard heads (unattentiveness) brings about a painful rear end!

Mothers teach, live, and practice the Golden Rules!

L to R: Ron, Mama, and Willie

L to R: Granddaughter, Melanie, Author, and Mama

Love, Love, Love!

Every girl will grow up to be a

Woman,

but not

Every woman will become

A lady!

L to R: Millie, Mama, and Author

L to R: Eddis, Author, Mama (seated), and Millie

L to R: Author, Mama, Monique, Eddis and Kelly

Mothers are

Guiding Lights

to

Long Health

and a

Fulfilling Life!

It's up to you!
Determine your course and stay focused.
Follow that which is Good!

Don't worry about the next person,

YOU just be right!

(Do what's right in the sight of God.)
You are responsible for your choices
and decisions in life.
The age of 12 has been known as
the age of accountability.

AN

IRREPLACEABLE

TREASURE!

"For where your treasure is, there will your heart be also."
Matthew 6:21

Who can replace a Godly mother?
Mothers are the groundkeepers of our soul.
Any woman can be called a mama, but not
every woman can be a Godly mother.

If you make a dime,

Save a nickel!

**"For the love of money is the root of all evil; which while
some coveted after, they have erred from the faith,
and pierced themselves through with many sorrows."
I Timothy 6:10**

Mothers always prepare and hope for a brighter future.
They do not settle for
"That'll do."

Teeth and Tongue

fall out, sometimes

You are what you speak;

Learn to tame the tongue!

Your thoughts influence

the tongue.

PRAY,

It will be alright in the morning!

His anger lasts only for a moment,

But his kindness lasts for a lifetime.

"Crying may last for a night, but joy comes in the morning."
Psalm 30:5

Prayer is the fluid that keeps the
Soul hydrated!

It keeps one in perfect peace.

A heart as

Boundless as

the

Universe

…

is defined as

"Mother"

"But sanctify the Lord God in your hearts; and be ready
always to give an answer to every man that asketh you a
reason of the hope that is in you with meekness and fear."
I Peter 3:15

Love never fails.
It starts with an awesome and <u>never</u> ends!

Create a winding road of love that can
interlock throughout your community.

You Don't Have to Look for

Mr. Right,

He'll find YOU!

"Whosoever findeth a wife, findeth a good thing,
and obtaineth favor of the Lord."
Proverb 18:22

Choose carefully

Who

<u>YOU</u>

<u>have Your</u>

Children by!

**"So give yourselves completely to God.
Stand against the devil, and the devil will run from you."
James 4:7**

Sins of the father – falls on the child/children

Don't always go by what you see;
you will be fooled most every time.
Seek the spirit of discernment.

Mothers are all time favorites in the book of LIFE.

**"Honour thy father and thy mother:
that thy days may be long upon the Land
which the LORD thy God giveth thee."
Exodus 20:12**

A mother's love is a precious jewel to illuminate light when help is needed!

Their love gets sweeter as the days go by.

Mothers are Life Long Teachers.

We are all somewhere between

YOUNG
&
OLD

India, Author and Monique

Mama and Melanie

3 Generations

Get up with Somebody that's Further along in Something than You!

"And Mary arose in those days, and went into the hill country with haste, into a city of Juda." Luke 1:39

Ruth followed Naomi

It's sad to know and know that you don't know, but even worse is to "don't know and don't know you don't know!"

Breath

and

Britches

"For which cause we faint not; but though our outward man perish, ye the inward man is renewed day by day."
2 Corinthians 4:16

They are helping to shape Our World.
They are standing tall.
Men and women are working together
for a better tomorrow!

*We will
Always
Love
Mama,
Big Ma
Biggs!*

*Such
Beautiful
Memories to
Cherish.*

To know Jesus is to have the

Supreme Remedy

for

All of our lack.

We are all in need of improvement
in some area of our lives.

Believing in God is the perfect assurance
of having the love and care always.

Mothers are

Door Keepers

to a

Whole

New World

Mothers are protectors and change makers.

They create, inspire, motivate, and
help to change the world.

Prayer Warriors

=

Mothers

"And Hannah prayed, and said, My heart rejoiceth in the Lord, mine horn is exalted in the Lord: my mouth is enlarged over mine enemies; because I rejoice in thy salvation." I Samuel 2:1

"They that were full have hired out themselves for bread; and they that hath many hungry ceased; so that the barren hath born seven; and she hath many children is waxed feeble." I Samuel 2:5

Mothers pray night and day.
Mothers never give up on their children!
They always have our back!

Mothers come in different

sizes and shapes

with

Much

Love

to give.

**"Ye are of God, little children, and have overcome them; because
greater is he that is in you, than He that is in the world." I John 4:4**

Large or small; short, big, or tall;
a Mother's Love says it ALL.
Every mother has a story to tell.

I Found the Answer

I

Learned

to

PRAY

"Be careful for nothing; but in everything by prayer
and supplication with Thanksgiving let your request
be made known unto God." Philippians 4:6

Seek and Develop

A

Personal

Relationship

With

GOD!

"Spend time with the wise and you will become wise,
but the friends of fools will suffer."
Proverbs 13:20

There is always enough time to give
thanks and be thankful.

There are no dumb questions,

Just

Dumb

Results

From

Not Asking!

Never be ashamed to not know something.

Erasers are on pencils to correct mistakes!

I'm a Cute Little Girl

I'm a Cute Little Figure,

Step back Boys,

Until I get a Little

Big.........ger.

"Wise children make their father happy,
but foolish children disrespect their mother."
Proverbs 15:20

YOUR

Character

Counts!

"What I tell you in darkness, that speak ye in light:
and what ye hear in the ear,
that preach ye upon the housetops."
Matthew 10:27

You are SOMEBODY!

Honor / Respect

Your Heritage

There is only ONE of you!
Know your roots!
Respect your elders!
Love Others!
Love Yourself!

When you help someone,
You're helping yourself!

No one can wear your hat for you!

It may not fit another's head.

Use Your Head

For more than

A Hat Rack!

Hats come in many styles and colors,
but we only have one head.

Cover your head to keep your brain in
function mode and your eyes clear to
minimize wrinkles on your forehead.

Thinking is a skill that requires
careful thought before acting.

Believe

In

Yourself

Always!

Be your #1 Fan!

Anything God created has worth!

God does not take

from one

to give to

Another!

**"Beloved I wish above all things that they
could prosper and be in good health."
3 John 1:2**

Remember God created heaven and earth.
He has the first and the last word. There is
enough in this world for any and everyone.

God designed us to give love,
not create hate.

Grateful
Grateful
Grateful
Grateful
Grateful
Grateful
Grateful
Grateful
Grateful
Grateful

Grate...ful...ness
for

Mother!

"The elder women as mothers;
the younger as sisters, with all purity."
I Timothy 5:2

H Honorable
Honeysuckle roses
with sweet nectar

E Emphasizes
Mothers feel
Everything

T Tenacious
Trustworthy

R The Rock
Resilient

MOTHERS
are an
extension of
God's Love

O Outstanding
Ombudsmen
out of this World!

S Super natural
Strong

M Magnificent
Magical
Make things happen

39

INDEX (BIBLIOGRAPHY)

p. xi   Proverbs 31, King James Version (KJV)

p. xiii   Webster Dictionary, definition of Wisdom

p. xiii   1 Thessalonians 5:11 – New International Version (NIV)

p. xiv   Great Women – Hallmark 2019

p. 1   Poem by Keats, A Thing of Beauty

p. 4   Philippians 4:13 – NIV

p. 6   Ephesians 2:19 – KJV

p. 13   Matthew 6:21 – KJV

p. 14   I Timothy 6:10 – KJV

p. 16   Psalm 30:5 – Life Connecting Bible (LCB)

p. 17   I Peter 3:15 – LCB

p. 18   Proverbs 18:22 – KJV

p. 19   James 4:7 – LCB

p. 20   Exodus 20:12 – KJV

p. 22   Luke 1:39 – KJV

p. 23   2 Corinthians 4:16 – KJV

p. 27   1 Samuel 2:1 – KJV

p. 27   1 Samuel 2:5 – KJV

p. 28   1 John 4:4 – KJV

p. 29   Philippians 4:6 – KJV

p. 30   Proverbs 13:20 – LCB

p. 32   Proverbs 15:20 – LCB

p. 33   Matthew 10:28 – KJV

p. 37   3 John 1:2 – LCB

p. 38   1 Timothy 5:2 – KJV

CPSIA information can be obtained
at www.ICGtesting.com
Printed in the USA
BVHW031147200519
548789BV00005B/786/P